Contents

Mr. Vinegar

By Joseph Jacobs

Mr. and Mrs. Vinegar lived in a vinegar bottle. Now, one day, when Mr. Vinegar was away from home, Mrs. Vinegar (who was a very good housewife) was busily sweeping her house when an unlucky thump of the broom brought the whole house clitter-clatter, clitter-clatter about her ears. In an agony of grief she rushed to meet her husband. Seeing

The Remarkable Rocket

and other silly stories

Compiled by Vic Parker

Miles
Kelly

First published in 2013 by Miles Kelly Publishing Ltd
Harding's Barn, Bardfield End Green, Thaxted, Essex, CM6 3PX, UK

2 4 6 8 10 9 7 5 3 1

Publishing Director Belinda Gallagher
Creative Director Jo Cowan
Editorial Director Rosie McGuire
Senior Editor Carly Blake
Editorial Assistant Amy Johnson
Designer Joe Jones
Production Manager Elizabeth Collins
Reprographics Stephan Davis, Jennifer Hunt, Thom Allaway

ISBN 978-1-84810-931-5

Printed in China

British Library Cataloging-in-Publication Data
A catalog record for this book is available from the British Library

ACKNOWLEDGMENTS
The publishers would like to thank the following artists who have contributed to this book:

Beehive Illustration Agency: Rosie Brooks, Mike Phillips
The Bright Agency: Michael Garton
Jan Lewis (inc. cover), Aimee Mappley (decorative frames)

All other artwork from the Miles Kelly Artwork Bank

Made with paper from a sustainable forest

www.mileskelly.net   info@mileskelly.net

www.factsforprojects.com

him she exclaimed, "Oh, Mr. Vinegar, Mr. Vinegar, we are ruined. I have knocked the house down. It is all to pieces!"

Mr. Vinegar then said, "My dear, let us see what can be done.

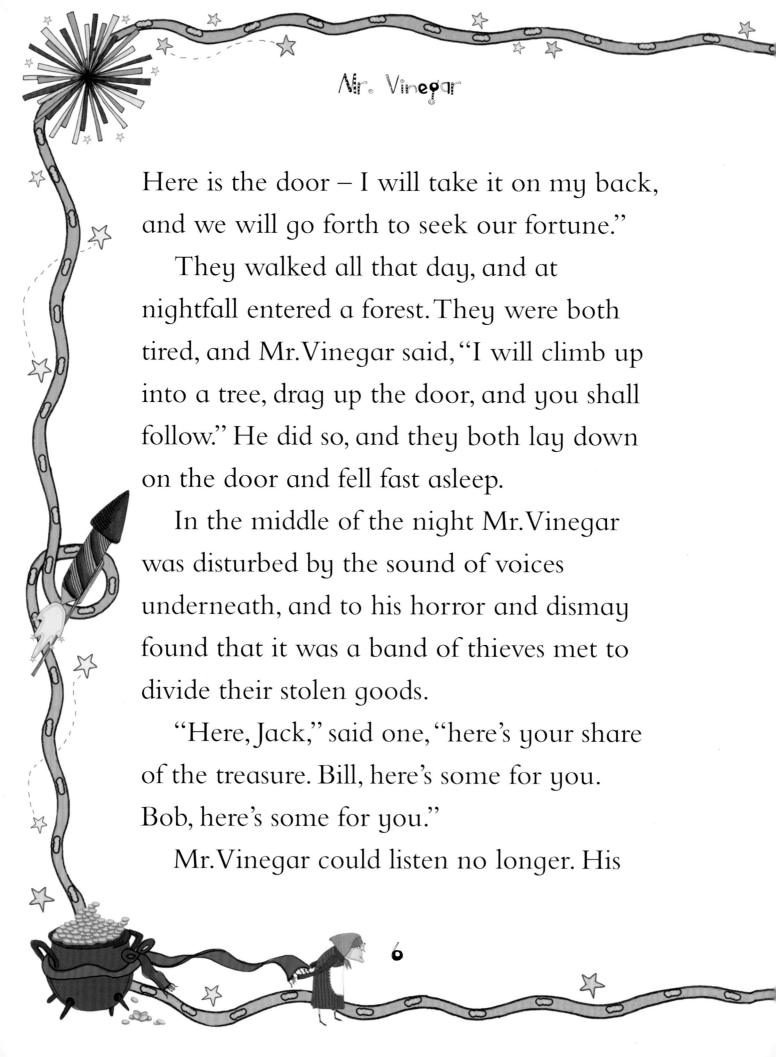

Here is the door – I will take it on my back, and we will go forth to seek our fortune."

They walked all that day, and at nightfall entered a forest. They were both tired, and Mr. Vinegar said, "I will climb up into a tree, drag up the door, and you shall follow." He did so, and they both lay down on the door and fell fast asleep.

In the middle of the night Mr. Vinegar was disturbed by the sound of voices underneath, and to his horror and dismay found that it was a band of thieves met to divide their stolen goods.

"Here, Jack," said one, "here's your share of the treasure. Bill, here's some for you. Bob, here's some for you."

Mr. Vinegar could listen no longer. His

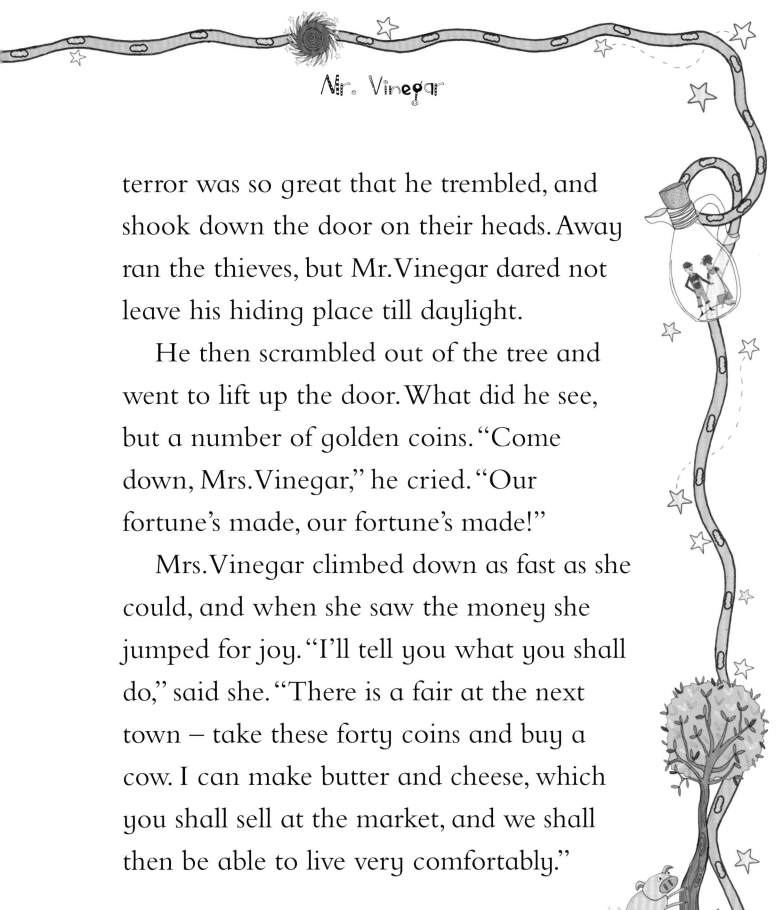

terror was so great that he trembled, and shook down the door on their heads. Away ran the thieves, but Mr. Vinegar dared not leave his hiding place till daylight.

He then scrambled out of the tree and went to lift up the door. What did he see, but a number of golden coins. "Come down, Mrs. Vinegar," he cried. "Our fortune's made, our fortune's made!"

Mrs. Vinegar climbed down as fast as she could, and when she saw the money she jumped for joy. "I'll tell you what you shall do," said she. "There is a fair at the next town – take these forty coins and buy a cow. I can make butter and cheese, which you shall sell at the market, and we shall then be able to live very comfortably."

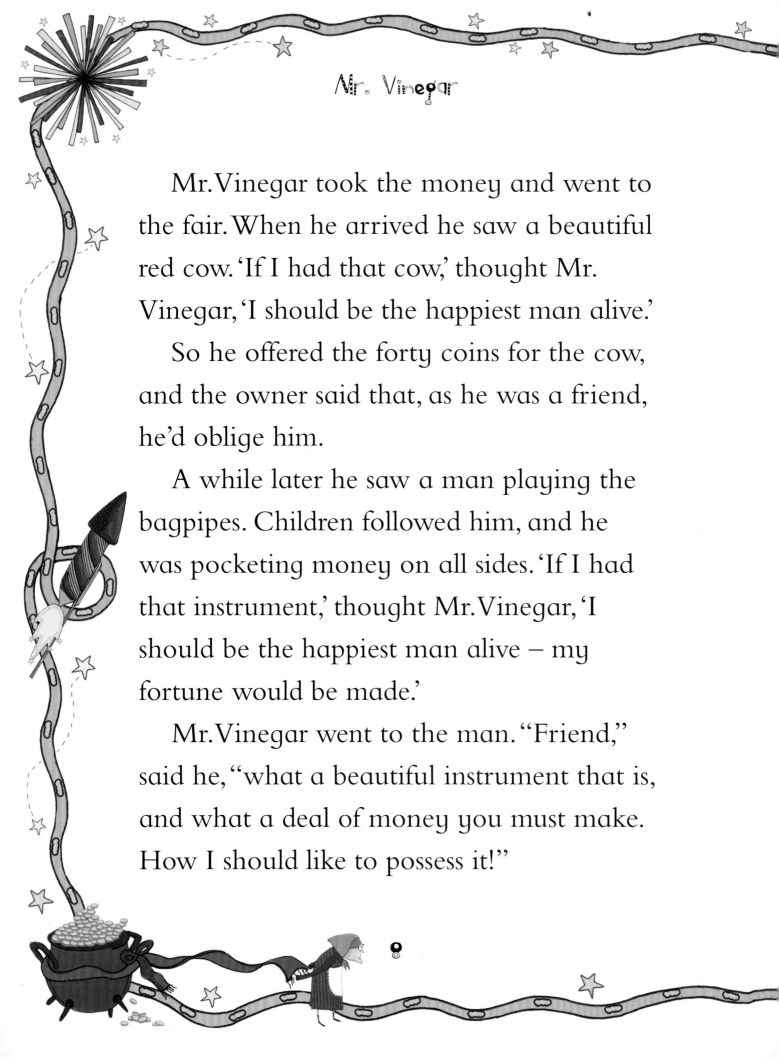

Mr. Vinegar

Mr. Vinegar took the money and went to the fair. When he arrived he saw a beautiful red cow. 'If I had that cow,' thought Mr. Vinegar, 'I should be the happiest man alive.'

So he offered the forty coins for the cow, and the owner said that, as he was a friend, he'd oblige him.

A while later he saw a man playing the bagpipes. Children followed him, and he was pocketing money on all sides. 'If I had that instrument,' thought Mr. Vinegar, 'I should be the happiest man alive – my fortune would be made.'

Mr. Vinegar went to the man. "Friend," said he, "what a beautiful instrument that is, and what a deal of money you must make. How I should like to possess it!"

"Well," said the man, "as you are a friend, I don't much mind parting with it. You shall have it for that red cow."

"Done!" said Mr. Vinegar. But it was in vain that he tried to play a tune. Instead of pocketing money, boys followed him, laughing and throwing things.

Poor Mr. Vinegar. His fingers grew cold. As he was leaving town, he met a man with a thick pair of gloves.

"Now if I had but those beautiful gloves, I should be the happiest man alive,"

9

said Mr. Vinegar to himself. He went up to the man, and said to him, "Friend, you seem to have a capital pair of gloves there."

"Yes," cried the man, "my hands are as warm as can be this cold November day."

"I should like to have them," said Mr. Vinegar."

"As you are a friend," said the man, "you can have them for those bagpipes."

"Done!" cried Mr. Vinegar. He put on the gloves and felt perfectly happy as he trudged homeward.

At last he grew very tired, when he saw a man coming toward him with a stout walking stick in his hand. "If I had but that stick," said Mr. Vinegar, "I should then be the happiest man alive." He said to the man: "Friend! What a good stick you have."

"Yes," said the man, "I have used it for many a long mile. As you are a friend, I don't mind giving it to you for those gloves."

Mr. Vinegar's hands were so warm, and his legs so tired, that he gladly agreed.

As he drew near to the wood, he heard a parrot in a tree calling out his name.

"Mr. Vinegar, you foolish man," mocked the parrot. "You went to the fair, and laid out all your money in buying a cow. Then you changed it for bagpipes, which were not worth one-tenth of the money. Then you changed the bagpipes for gloves, which were not worth one-quarter of the money. And then you changed the gloves for a miserable stick. And now for your forty coins, cow, bagpipes and gloves, you have nothing but that stick, which you might have cut in a hedge."

Mr. Vinegar, falling into a rage, threw the stick at the parrot's head. The stick lodged in the tree, and he returned to his wife without money, cow, bagpipes, gloves or stick. She gave him such a sound scolding that he never did anything quite so silly again.

The Moon-Cake

Edited by Hamilton Wright Mabie,
Edward Everett Hale and
William Byron Forbush

A little boy had a cake that a big boy really wanted for himself. The greedy lad thought hard, wondering how he could get the cake without making the little boy cry, for then surely it would attract his mother's attention and she would see what was going on. Just in time, as the little boy held up the cake to his lips to take a bite, the big boy hit on an idea.

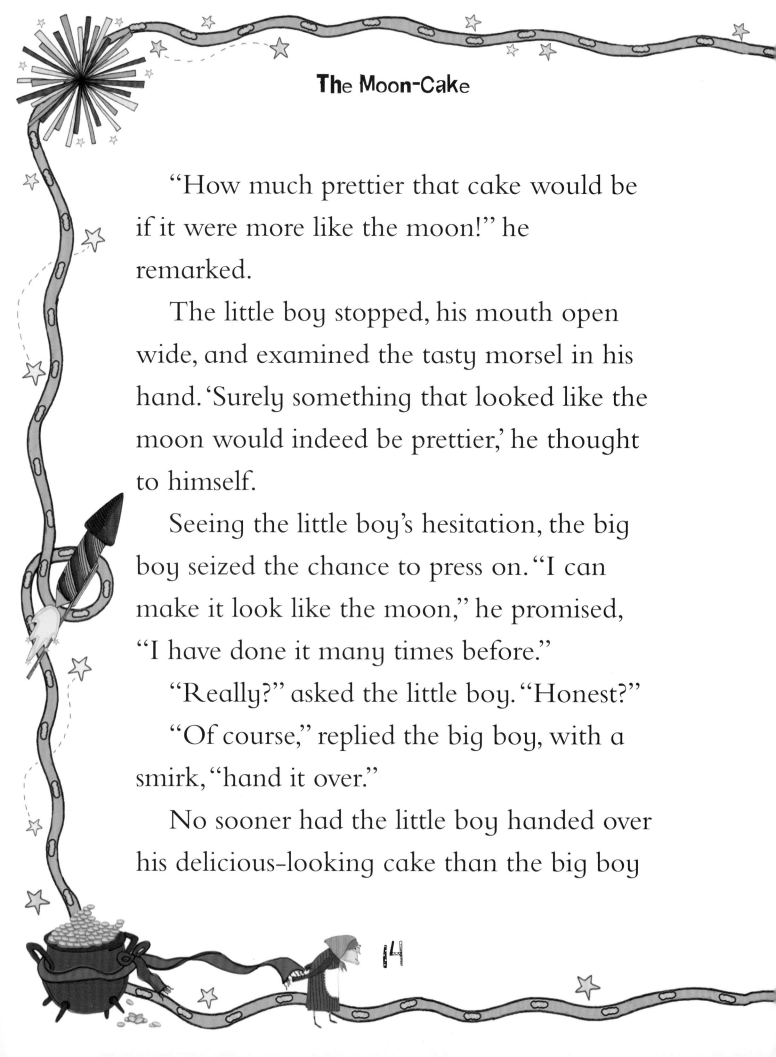

"How much prettier that cake would be if it were more like the moon!" he remarked.

The little boy stopped, his mouth open wide, and examined the tasty morsel in his hand. 'Surely something that looked like the moon would indeed be prettier,' he thought to himself.

Seeing the little boy's hesitation, the big boy seized the chance to press on. "I can make it look like the moon," he promised, "I have done it many times before."

"Really?" asked the little boy. "Honest?"

"Of course," replied the big boy, with a smirk, "hand it over."

No sooner had the little boy handed over his delicious-looking cake than the big boy

took out a mouthful, leaving a crescent with a jagged edge.

"Nooooooo!" cried out the little boy, beginning to whimper and trying to grab back the cake.

Holding it out of his reach the big boy hastily urged, "Don't worry – I'll make it better. I'll neaten it up into a half-moon." So saying, he nibbled off the horns of the crescent, and gnawed the edge smooth.

15

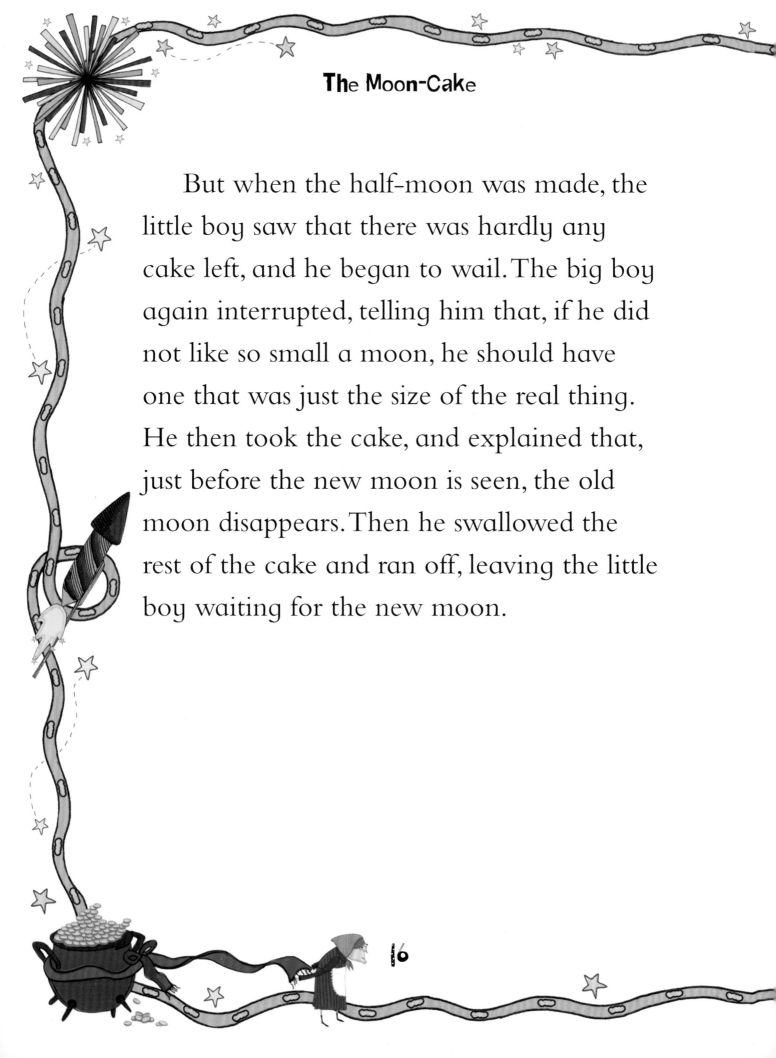

The Moon-Cake

But when the half-moon was made, the little boy saw that there was hardly any cake left, and he began to wail. The big boy again interrupted, telling him that, if he did not like so small a moon, he should have one that was just the size of the real thing. He then took the cake, and explained that, just before the new moon is seen, the old moon disappears. Then he swallowed the rest of the cake and ran off, leaving the little boy waiting for the new moon.

The Remarkable Rocket

By Oscar Wilde

The King's son was going to be married, so there was great rejoicing. He had waited a whole year for his bride, and at last she had arrived. She was a Russian princess, and had driven all the way from Finland in a sleigh drawn by reindeer. The sleigh was shaped like a great golden swan, and between the swan's wings lay the Princess herself. Her long ermine cloak reached

17

down to her feet, on her head was a tiny silver cap and she was as pale as the Snow Palace in which she had always lived. As she drove through the streets all the people threw down flowers on her from the balconies.

At the gate of the castle the Prince was waiting to receive her. When he saw her he sank upon one knee, and kissed her hand. "Your picture was beautiful," he murmured, "but you are more beautiful than your picture." The Princess blushed.

When the day for the marriage arrived, it was a magnificent ceremony. The bride and bridegroom walked hand in hand under a canopy of purple velvet embroidered with little pearls. Then there

was a state banquet, which lasted for five hours. The Prince and Princess sat at the top of the Great Hall and drank out of a cup of clear crystal.

After the banquet there was a ball. The bride and bridegroom were to dance the Rose-dance together, and the King played the flute. He played very badly, but no one dared to tell him so because he was the King. Indeed, everybody cried out, "Charming! Charming!"

The last item on the program was a grand display of fireworks, to be let off exactly at midnight. The little Princess had never seen a firework in her life and was most excited. At the end of the King's garden a great stand had been set up. As

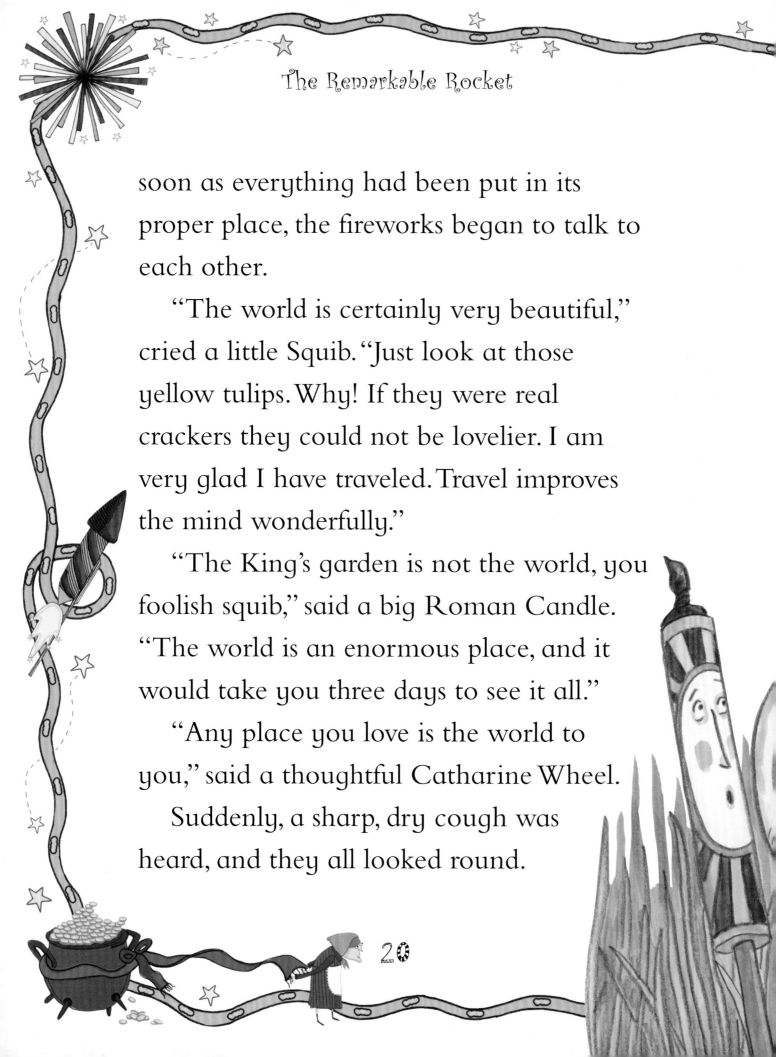

soon as everything had been put in its proper place, the fireworks began to talk to each other.

"The world is certainly very beautiful," cried a little Squib. "Just look at those yellow tulips. Why! If they were real crackers they could not be lovelier. I am very glad I have traveled. Travel improves the mind wonderfully."

"The King's garden is not the world, you foolish squib," said a big Roman Candle. "The world is an enormous place, and it would take you three days to see it all."

"Any place you love is the world to you," said a thoughtful Catharine Wheel.

Suddenly, a sharp, dry cough was heard, and they all looked round.

It came from a tall, haughty-looking
Rocket, who was tied to the end of
a long stick.

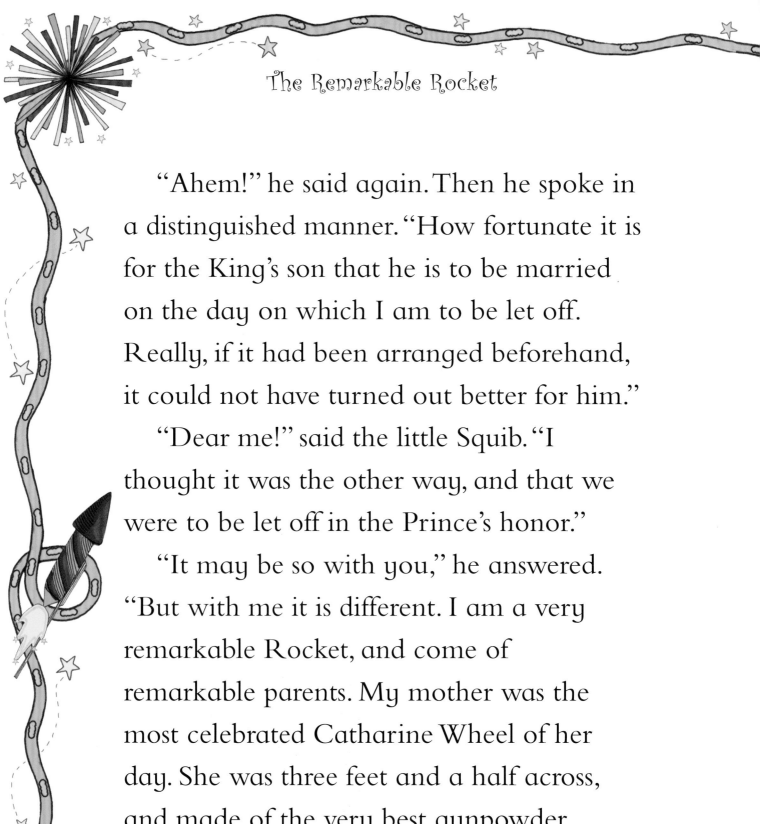

"Ahem!" he said again. Then he spoke in a distinguished manner. "How fortunate it is for the King's son that he is to be married on the day on which I am to be let off. Really, if it had been arranged beforehand, it could not have turned out better for him."

"Dear me!" said the little Squib. "I thought it was the other way, and that we were to be let off in the Prince's honor."

"It may be so with you," he answered. "But with me it is different. I am a very remarkable Rocket, and come of remarkable parents. My mother was the most celebrated Catharine Wheel of her day. She was three feet and a half across, and made of the very best gunpowder.

"My father was a Rocket like myself,"

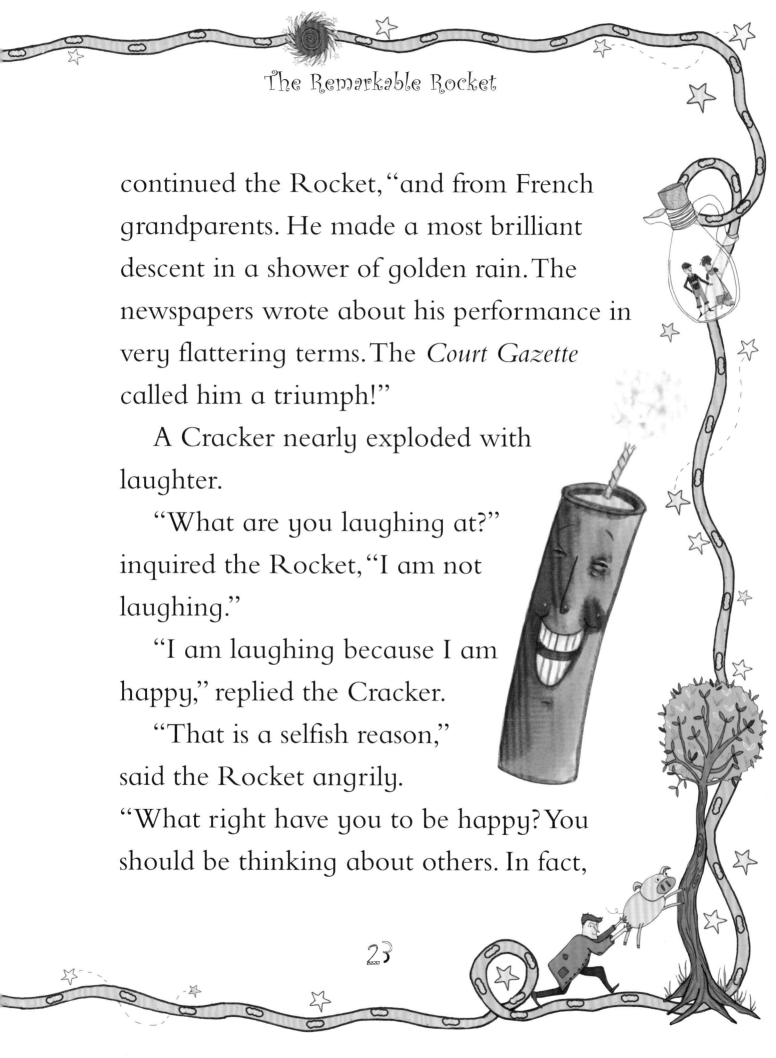

continued the Rocket, "and from French grandparents. He made a most brilliant descent in a shower of golden rain. The newspapers wrote about his performance in very flattering terms. The *Court Gazette* called him a triumph!"

A Cracker nearly exploded with laughter.

"What are you laughing at?" inquired the Rocket, "I am not laughing."

"I am laughing because I am happy," replied the Cracker.

"That is a selfish reason," said the Rocket angrily. "What right have you to be happy? You should be thinking about others. In fact, you should be thinking about me. I am always thinking about myself, and I expect everybody else to do the same. Suppose, for instance, anything happened to me tonight. The Prince and Princess would never be happy again – and as for the King, I know he would not get over it. When I think about the importance of my position, I am almost moved to tears."

"If you want to give pleasure to others," cried the Roman Candle, "you had better keep yourself dry."

"Certainly," exclaimed the Bengal Light. "That is only common sense."

"Common sense, indeed!" said the Rocket indignantly. "You forget that I am uncommon, and very remarkable. Besides,

24

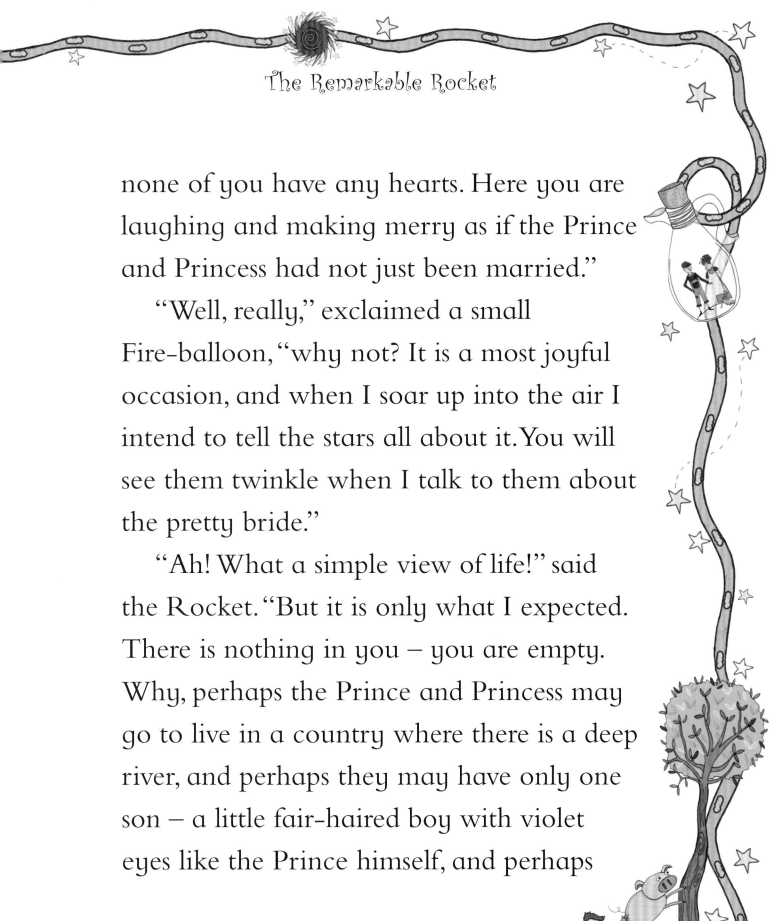

none of you have any hearts. Here you are laughing and making merry as if the Prince and Princess had not just been married."

"Well, really," exclaimed a small Fire-balloon, "why not? It is a most joyful occasion, and when I soar up into the air I intend to tell the stars all about it. You will see them twinkle when I talk to them about the pretty bride."

"Ah! What a simple view of life!" said the Rocket. "But it is only what I expected. There is nothing in you – you are empty. Why, perhaps the Prince and Princess may go to live in a country where there is a deep river, and perhaps they may have only one son – a little fair-haired boy with violet eyes like the Prince himself, and perhaps some day he may go out to walk with his nurse, and perhaps the nurse may go to sleep under a great elder tree, and perhaps the little boy may fall into the river and be drowned. What a terrible misfortune! Poor people, to lose their only son! It is really too dreadful! I shall never get over it."

"But they have not lost their only son," said the Roman Candle.

"I never said that they had," replied the Rocket. "I said that they might. I hate people who cry over spilt milk. But when I think that they might lose their only son, I certainly am very much affected."

"You certainly are!" cried the Bengal Light. "In fact, you are the most affected person I ever met."

"You are the rudest person I ever met," said the Rocket, offended.

"You had really better keep yourself dry," said the Fire-balloon. "That is the important thing."

"Important for you," answered the Rocket, "but I shall weep if I choose." And he actually burst into real tears, which flowed down his stick like raindrops. They nearly drowned two little beetles who were just thinking of setting up house.

Then the moon rose

27

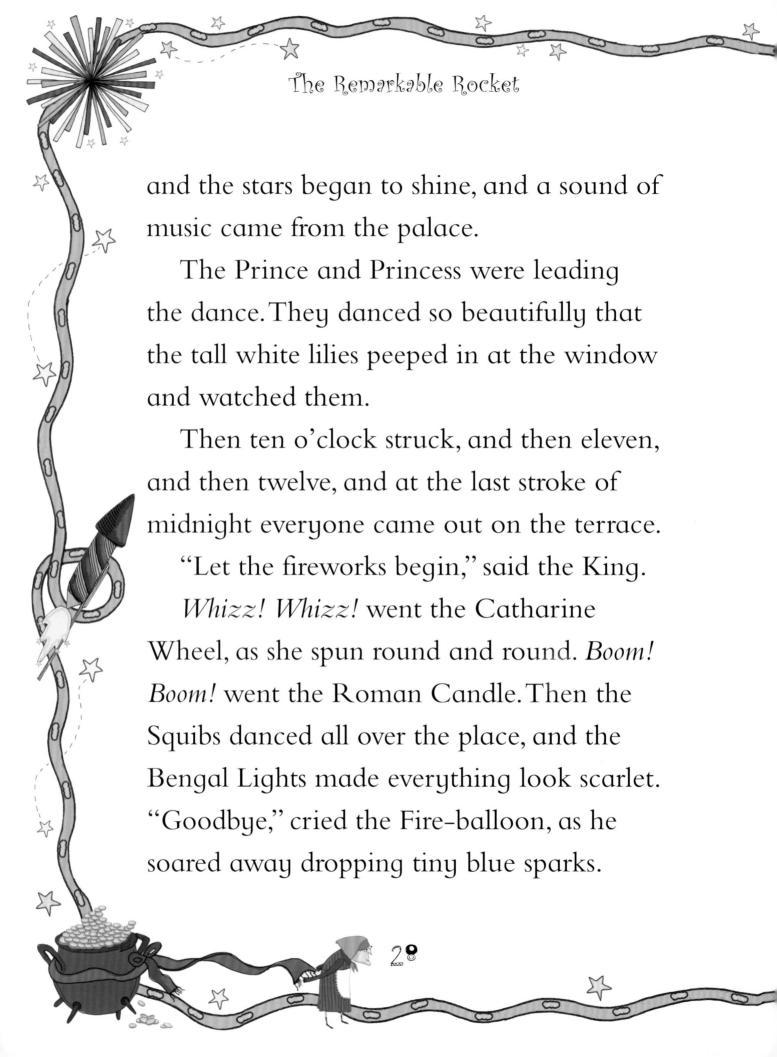

and the stars began to shine, and a sound of music came from the palace.

The Prince and Princess were leading the dance. They danced so beautifully that the tall white lilies peeped in at the window and watched them.

Then ten o'clock struck, and then eleven, and then twelve, and at the last stroke of midnight everyone came out on the terrace.

"Let the fireworks begin," said the King.

Whizz! Whizz! went the Catharine Wheel, as she spun round and round. *Boom! Boom!* went the Roman Candle. Then the Squibs danced all over the place, and the Bengal Lights made everything look scarlet. "Goodbye," cried the Fire-balloon, as he soared away dropping tiny blue sparks.

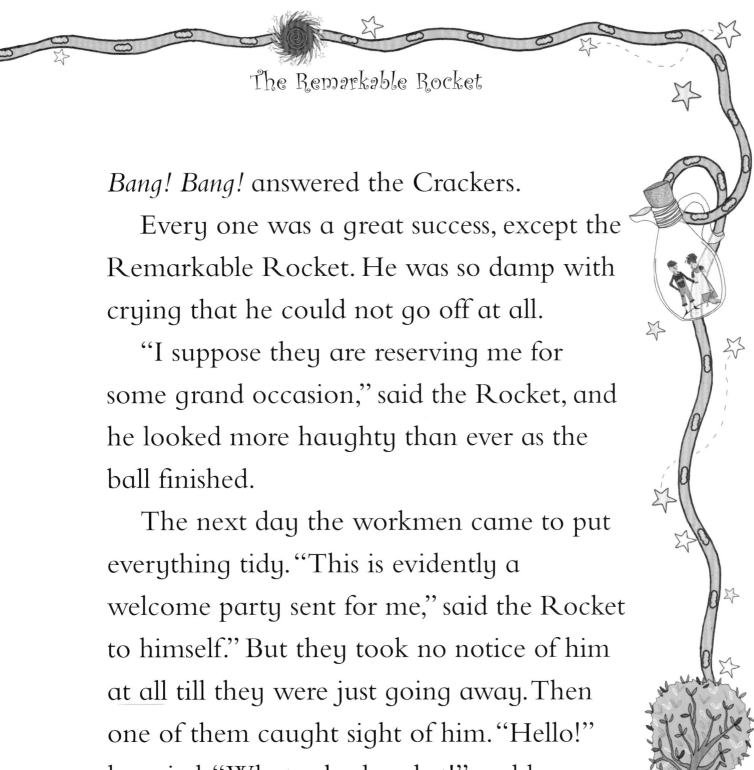

Bang! Bang! answered the Crackers.

Every one was a great success, except the Remarkable Rocket. He was so damp with crying that he could not go off at all.

"I suppose they are reserving me for some grand occasion," said the Rocket, and he looked more haughty than ever as the ball finished.

The next day the workmen came to put everything tidy. "This is evidently a welcome party sent for me," said the Rocket to himself." But they took no notice of him at all till they were just going away. Then one of them caught sight of him. "Hello!" he cried, "What a bad rocket!" and he threw him over the wall into the ditch.

"*Bad* Rocket? *Bad* Rocket?" said the

Rocket as he whirled through the air. "Impossible! *Grand* Rocket, that is what the man said," and he fell into the mud.

After some time a large white duck swam by. She had yellow legs and webbed feet, and was considered a great beauty on account of her waddle.

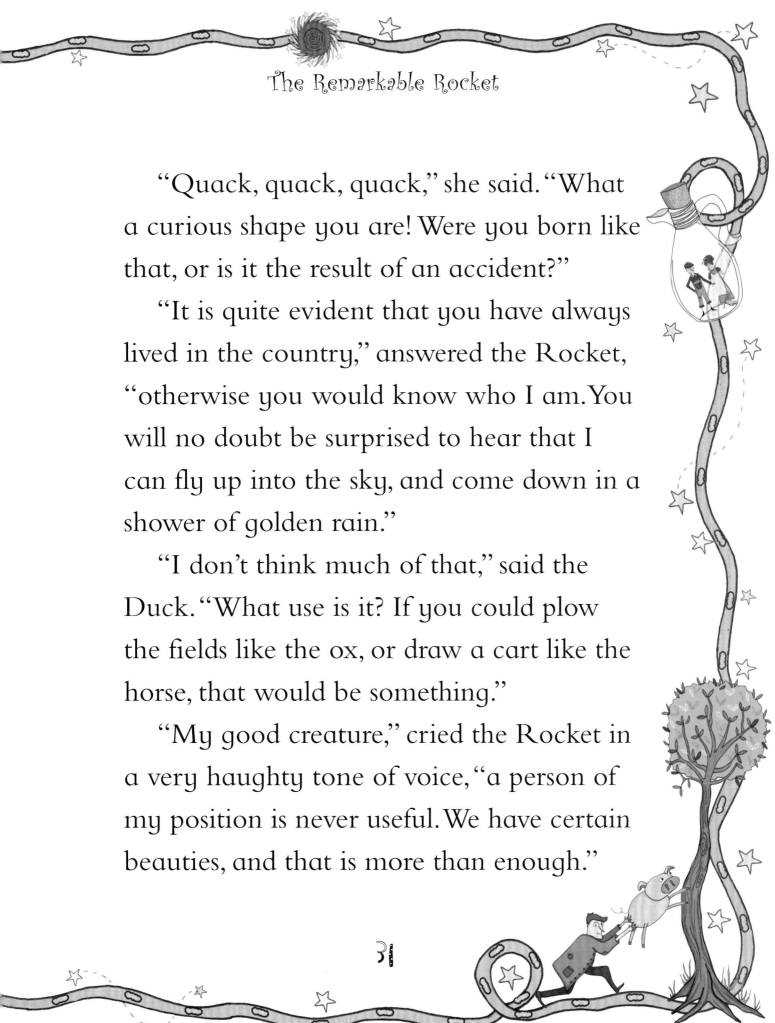

"Quack, quack, quack," she said. "What a curious shape you are! Were you born like that, or is it the result of an accident?"

"It is quite evident that you have always lived in the country," answered the Rocket, "otherwise you would know who I am. You will no doubt be surprised to hear that I can fly up into the sky, and come down in a shower of golden rain."

"I don't think much of that," said the Duck. "What use is it? If you could plow the fields like the ox, or draw a cart like the horse, that would be something."

"My good creature," cried the Rocket in a very haughty tone of voice, "a person of my position is never useful. We have certain beauties, and that is more than enough."

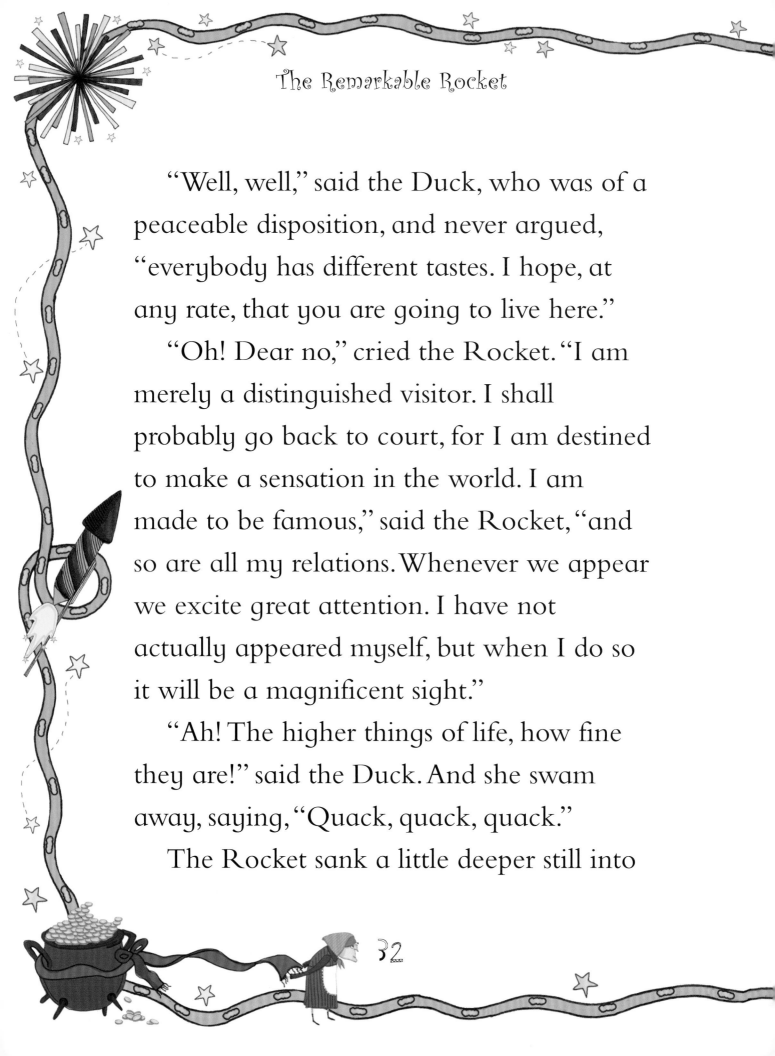

"Well, well," said the Duck, who was of a peaceable disposition, and never argued, "everybody has different tastes. I hope, at any rate, that you are going to live here."

"Oh! Dear no," cried the Rocket. "I am merely a distinguished visitor. I shall probably go back to court, for I am destined to make a sensation in the world. I am made to be famous," said the Rocket, "and so are all my relations. Whenever we appear we excite great attention. I have not actually appeared myself, but when I do so it will be a magnificent sight."

"Ah! The higher things of life, how fine they are!" said the Duck. And she swam away, saying, "Quack, quack, quack."

The Rocket sank a little deeper still into

the mud, when suddenly two little boys came running down the bank with a kettle and a bundle of sticks for making a fire. "Hello!" cried one of the boys. "Look at this old stick! I wonder how it came here."

"*Old* stick!" said the Rocket indignantly. "Impossible! *Gold* stick, that is what he said. *Gold* stick is very complimentary."

"Let us put it into the fire!" said the boy.

So they piled the sticks together, put the Rocket on top, and lit the fire.

"This is magnificent," cried the Rocket, "they are going to let me off in broad daylight, so that everyone can see me."

"We will go to sleep now," the boys said, "and when we wake up the kettle will be boiled."

The Rocket was very damp, so he took a long time to burn. At last, however, the fire caught him.

"Now I am going off!" he cried, and he made himself very stiff and straight. "I know I shall go much higher than the stars, much higher than the moon, much higher than the sun. In fact, I shall go so high that—"

Fizz! Fizz! Fizz! and he went straight up into the air.

"Delightful!" he cried. "I shall go on like this forever. What a success I am!"

But nobody saw him.

Then he began to feel a curious tingling sensation all over him.

"Now I am going to explode," he

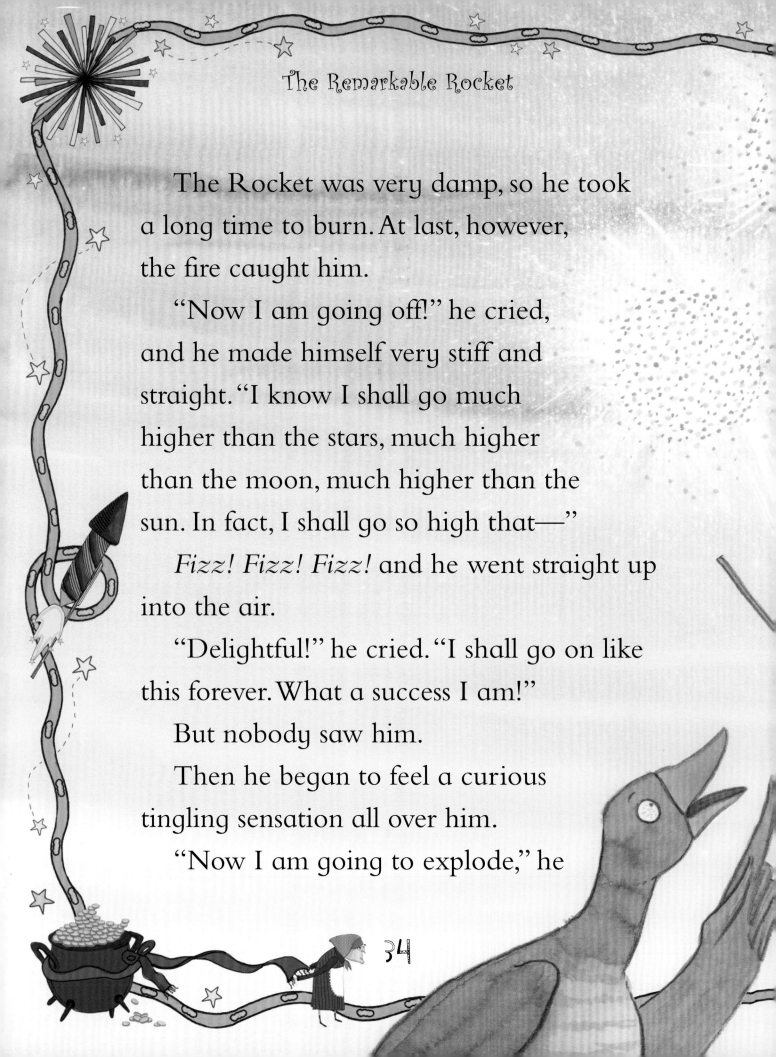

cried. "I shall set the whole world on fire and make such a noise that nobody will talk about anything else for a year." *Bang! Bang! Bang!* went the gunpowder. There was no doubt about it.

But nobody heard him, not even the two little boys, for they were sound asleep.

Then all that was left of him was the stick, and this fell down on the back of a Goose who was walking by the ditch.

"Good heavens!" cried the Goose. "It is raining sticks," and she went into the water.

"I knew I should create a big sensation," gasped the Rocket, and he went out.

A Visitor from Paradise

By Joseph Jacobs

There was once a woman, good but simple, whose first husband died, so she married again. One day, when her second husband was out in the fields, a tramp came by and asked for some water. She handed it to him, and asked where he came from.

"From Paris," said the man.

36

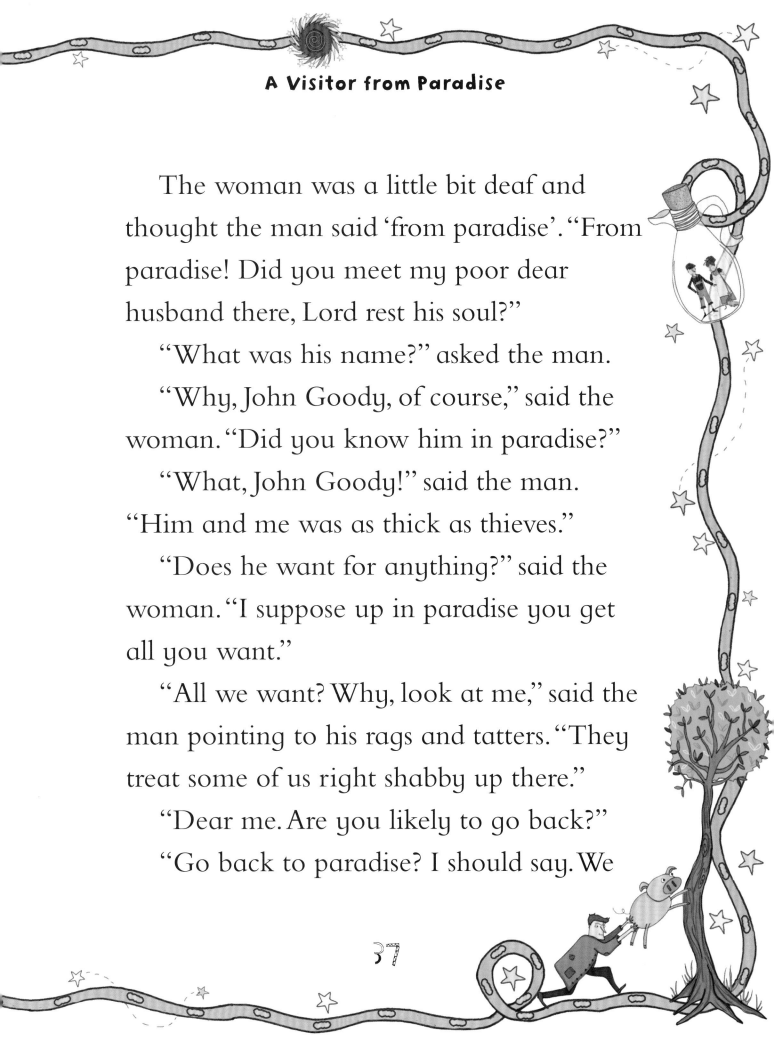

The woman was a little bit deaf and thought the man said 'from paradise'. "From paradise! Did you meet my poor dear husband there, Lord rest his soul?"

"What was his name?" asked the man.

"Why, John Goody, of course," said the woman. "Did you know him in paradise?"

"What, John Goody!" said the man. "Him and me was as thick as thieves."

"Does he want for anything?" said the woman. "I suppose up in paradise you get all you want."

"All we want? Why, look at me," said the man pointing to his rags and tatters. "They treat some of us right shabby up there."

"Dear me. Are you likely to go back?"

"Go back to paradise? I should say. We

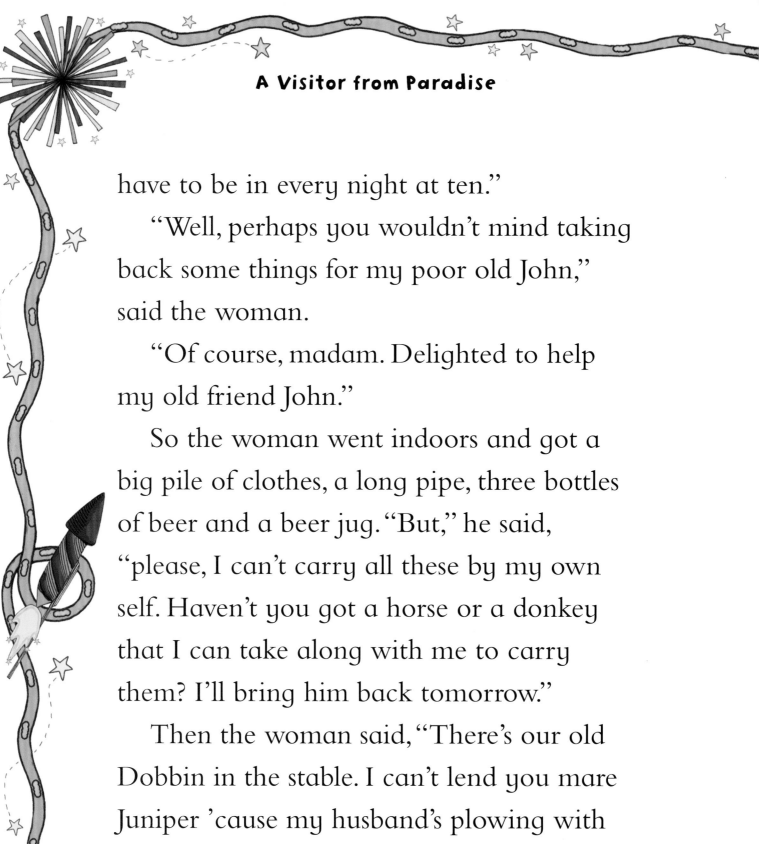

have to be in every night at ten."

"Well, perhaps you wouldn't mind taking back some things for my poor old John," said the woman.

"Of course, madam. Delighted to help my old friend John."

So the woman went indoors and got a big pile of clothes, a long pipe, three bottles of beer and a beer jug. "But," he said, "please, I can't carry all these by my own self. Haven't you got a horse or a donkey that I can take along with me to carry them? I'll bring him back tomorrow."

Then the woman said, "There's our old Dobbin in the stable. I can't lend you mare Juniper 'cause my husband's plowing with her just now."

"Ah, well, Dobbin'll do as it's only until tomorrow." The woman got out Dobbin and saddled him, and the man took the clothes, pipe and beer, then rode off. Afterward the woman's husband came home and said, "Where's Dobbin? He's not in the stable."

His wife told him what had happened. He said, "How do we know that he is going to paradise? That he'll bring Dobbin back tomorrow? I'll saddle Juniper and get our things back. Which way did he go?"

So her husband rode after the man, who saw him coming and guessed what had happened. He got off from Dobbin and drove him into some trees, then went and laid down and looked up to the sky. The farmer came up to him and said, "What are you doing there?"

"A funny thing," said the man. "A fellow came along on a horse with some clothes and things, and when he got to the top of the hill the horse went right up into the sky."

"Oh, it's all right then," said the farmer. "He's gone to paradise, sure enough."

Next day they waited for the man to bring back Dobbin, but he didn't come.

And they are still waiting.